And the cloudscapes.
Oh, the majestically empty cloudscapes.

(excerpt "Freefall")
~ James & Jose

Other Collabs
by Matthew Jose and Candice James

Double Trouble Volume I is the first of the series,
but as this flies off the shelves do not worry my friend,
there will be many more volumes to come!

Double Trouble Vol. I
poems from the edge

by

Matthew Jose
&
Candice James

Silver Bow Publishing
720 Sixth Street, Unit #5,
New Westminster, BC Canada
V3L3C5

Title: Double Trouble Vol I
Authors: Matthew Jose and Candice James
Publisher: Silver Bow Publishing
Cover Art: 'Fu Manchu and Father Exit the Building' painting by Candice James
Back Cover Art: 'Sky Trilogy' painting by Candice James
Cover Design: Candice James
Layout and editing: Candice James

97817741636 Print
97817741643 epub

Library and Archives Canada Cataloguing in Publication

Title: Double trouble. vol. I : poems from the edge / by Matthew Jose & Candice James.
Names: Jose, Matthew, 1976- author. | James, Candice, 1948- author.
Identifiers: Canadiana (print) 20210150289 | Canadiana (ebook) 20210150335 | ISBN 9781774031636
   (softcover) | ISBN 9781774031643 (EPUB)
Classification: LCC PS3610.075 D68 2021 | DDC 811/.6—dc23

To all the dreamers who realize
they are the dream being dreamt.

~ Matthew Jose & Candice James

Contents

Just Past the Road Not Taken ... 9
A Likely Story ... 10
A Line Here a LineThere ... 11
A-Bit about O-Bit-uaries ... 12
Afternoon Midnight Gambler ... 14
Changing Faces and Places ... 15
Dark Carnival ... 16
Do Ya Feel Lucky Punk? ... 17
High on a Limoncello Sea ... 19
Professor Barfly ... 20
Soup Du Jour ... 22
The Merciless Years ... 23
Who Knew? ... 24
Kind of, Sort of, Maybe ... 26
The Strive ... 27
Worry Not ... 28
Gulls Circling ... 29
Covid, Impeachments, Insurrection and the Steal ... 30
Mebbee, Mebbee Not ... 31
Ramble on Baby ... 33
The Big Shake Off ... 35
Shackles ... 36
Clear Cut Corners ... 37
That Damned Hole ... 38
The Big Questions ... 40
The Mystic ... 41
Wishes ... 42
The Quantum Matrix of My Mind ... 43
Freefall ... 45
Run Boy Run ... 47
The Bliss ... 49
Feelin' It and Knowin' It ... 50
The Numbers of Timeless Time ... 52

A Glorious Nonsense *(aka Sanostat Evidaris)* ... 54
The Power Behind These Moments ... 56
Yes Indeedie! ... 57
Long Gone ... 58
Stray Dogs ... 59
Monochromatic Calico ... 60
The Speaking Universe ... 61
Looking Back ... 64
Mind Stylus ... 65
Cycles ... 67
Embrace the Emptiness ... 68
We Are Not in Babylon ... 70
Samadhi Goals ... 71
Right There for the Taking ... 73
These Words ... 75
Puzzling ... 76
A Conversation with Stephen ... 77
Blue Herring ... 79
Evolver ... 81
The Poem Lives ... 83

Authors Profile ... 85

Just Past the Road Not Taken

Just past the road not taken,
I wandered in aimless circles
inside a square maze of indecision.
I came to an opening that offered no direction.

I traveled on in the clutch of uncertainty
with hope riding shotgun on my shoulders.

Then I stopped the journey
I sat on a smooth stone on a rocky road.

All I had left was the poem in my heart.
So, I picked up a shard of bone
and a remnant of buffalo hide.
I had no ink so I punctured my skin
and wrote with the blood of my soul.

Just past the road not taken
I became a poet.

A Likely Story

It's like the story of the guy
who got way ahead and then gave it all back,
just for the fun of it.
Or the guy who was forged in the image of a loser,
but ended up atop many a podium in his day.
Or the gal who purposely engaged in
the most damning of arguments
just to hustle them off.
But for me, too much and not enough
always amounted to the same thing.

Or maybe it's like the story of the writer,
who wrote too many chapters then tore them up,
to start a new fire
Or the poet who imprisoned rhyme on every line
then found the key to turn them into free verse.
Or the musician who shaped every note into staccato
Then slowed them down to legato.
But for me, the fire was always too cold,
The keys never fit and the fast was always too slow.

Or perhaps it's like the story of the punch drunk,
wayward, former heavyweight champ
who knew he took too many fights at the end of his career.
Or the professor who made his students buy his book,
every semester just to tickle his fancy.
Or the medieval bar wench, who, far ahead of her time,
realized women would one day rule a vast empire,
but kept that to herself for personal reasons.
But for me, when the bare smokescreens of nonsense
run away like the wild horses of Sable Island,
a truth, undisputable and obvious, often reveals itself,
and unfolds, like ... a likely story.

A Line Here. - A Line There

It's starting to feel like there's an air to it all,
in the emptiness of this atmosphere.
And an easiness too but that's secondary, really,
in my shortlist of primary things.
A dream in hand, a dream to spare.
A line here, a line there.

In awe of those who don't mind much burning,
I walk the empty streets watching the people,
yearning and turning and churning,
torn and small and box-like.
How do they get that way?
How did any of us get the way we are?
A line here, a line there.

I would blame my gentle center,
but nobody likes playing the blame game.
Nobody likes wearing the shame-name,
especially Mary Jane...a bit of a self-proclaimed saint.
She was a great old girl filled wish wisdom's strife,
helped me write my life.
A line here, a line there.

I guess it all just adds up to living,
for whatever that's worth.
Maybe we should look beyond even the masters' work,
for an even truer truth. Or maybe, just maybe ...
we should just close our eyes and dream:
another line here, another line there.

A-Bit about O-Bit-uaries

I was reading the obituaries the other day.
Not because I had lost someone in my life.
It's more like a hobby I enjoy doing in my free time.
Reading the cliff notes of random strangers' lives.
Reading what those who knew them best
thought were the most important,
or interesting parts of who they were.

It gets me to thinking about my own inevitable obituary.
If I'm lucky enough to have one written for me.
What would it say?
Maybe we all should just write our own obituaries,
while we are still alive.
I mean, who knows us better than ourselves?
Mine might read like this:

— Begin Obit

He spiraled and spun against the grain
to a musical score of his own creation,
to the ever-changing metronome in his mind.
He was political in his own unique way:
stumbling far right of mainstream,
tumbling far left of mundane.
His greatest regret was, although he was called *Professor*,
he never did receive his certificate from the academia.

End Obit

Yeah, maybe it would sound something like that.
Maybe it would say I lived to be old and forgettable.
Maybe it would say I yawned way too often.
Maybe it would say I was too simple,
too honest and too full of passion.

More than anything I hope it says
I played the hand I'd been dealt
with a card shark's zeal.

Footnote

Every moment should matter.
But most of us can't wrap our minds around that.
Myself included, more times than I care to admit.

So here's to the hills and the valleys
and all the space that lies between.
And here's to any soul brave enough to ante up.

Afternoon Midnight Gambler

You know what will really get those horses moving?
It could never be the paper alone.
The Racing Form is one thing
and the heavy-duty bookie is another,
but getting carried away on this addiction
of 4 legged burners tearing up the track
is a horse of a different colour
and another thing altogether.
Just ask the afternoon midnight gambler.

You know what will really get you thinking?
It'll never be the tick-tock monkey master in your mind.
Monkey business and glad handing are one thing,
and the newbie day trader
on the exchange floor is another.

But betting it all on a sure winner *(not)*
and throwing caution and cash to the wind
is a ticket to 'Bleak House Alley' or the asylum.
It's never a *Ticket to Ride.*
It's just a Ringo-type crushed *Beatle,*
stuck to the bottom of your shoe,
and dragged into the house.
It's a dog-eared Ace of Clubs,
headed for the trash can.
Just ask the afternoon midnight gambler ...
Just ask me.

Changing Faces and Places

I'm an outlaw riding through the night,
with a trigger finger itching to pull,
and a posse of derelict cops
chasing me from one bar to another
in this rabbit hole dream I'm stuck in.

I blow the swinging doors wide open.
I set myself and my money down hard
and order a double, single-malt scotch.
I line myself up in the bar-length mirror,
surreptitiously pull my slouch hat down.
Just another face behind the bottles ...
That's the way I like it.

Seconds are only a fragmented memory,
and minutes refuse to take my call,
and this dream keeps changing faces and places
in the hours I spend, wasted, in this oasis.

Then out of nowhere, as if she can read my thoughts,
the beautiful bar-maiden whispers in my ear,
"will you accept some of this?"
Without missing a beat, I reply,
"Baby, I'll take whatever you have to offer,
and I'll take it good."
One of those *'I'm fairly pleased with myself'* smiles
begins to broaden my mouth's horizon,
as she pours me a another double
with a side of the most beautiful eyes I've ever seen.

These are the moments that count, I think to myself.
These are the moments to savor and keep tucked away,
to take the edge off a butcher-knife day
after the dream changes faces and places.

Dark Carnival

If there is frenzy in the world,
and wreckage at sea,
I can't imagine it being more chaotic
than this dream I am dreaming tonight.

I lie in the covert hold,
of that cagey old trickster, time,
recklessly riding high on a galloping seahorse
approaching a dangerous shoreline,
laughing and dancing maniacally
because I have no weapons to defend against
this untimely intrusion of long-lost time.

That cagey old fool is a trick in my mind
and I'm the one-trick pony
that performs its dark carnival to death,
in the ditch of my bated and wasted breath.

But a one-trick pony is better
than a no-trick pony.
And dusty self-talk is good company
in no-man's-land.

Remember, there usually aren't enough seats
in the lifeboats
and a life-jacket only works
if you're wearing it.

And, more importantly,
it's time I got out of this dream
and quit this dark carnival for good.

So, I trip up to the sky
waving with a fading yell,
'Bye ... I'll write soon ...'
... knowing I won't.

Do Ya Feel Lucky Punk?

To a certain extent we've all lucked it,
more times than we probably realize.

Based on the chances of it happening,
your birth is miraculous.
Based on the chances of it happening,
your death is imminent.
But the fact that any of us
ere even invited onto the ride
is mind boggling.

If you've ever seen the ocean in person …
you've lucked it.
If you've ever seen a child take their first steps …
you've lucked it.

But always, there has to be unlucky ones,

Based on the unfair tipping of circumstance,
a million tears will fall tonight.
Based on the cruel winds of change,
a million hearts will break tonight.
But the fact is, tears and heartache are what shape us
and make us the cats or dogs we are.

If you've ever loved and lost …
you've un-lucked it.
If you've ever watched a dream die …
you've un-lucked it.

The lucky and the unlucky …
Park Avenue and the Bronx.
Shake 'em up in a blender:
See how they like the other side.
See how they handle the slide of the tumbling dice.
See if they're naughty or nice,
or if they're still on Santa's list.

Miracles and horrors are all part of the ride.
We don't get to choose the ratio
we'll be forced to endure.

But we do choose:
Which worm will be placed on the fishing hook.
Which songs to sing while intoxicated.
And whether we're still willing to show love
in the hard times.

Today's a new day
and I'm loaded for bear,
stakin' my claim to luck it!

If you see me comin'
and I ain't smilin' ...
better step aside fool,
and if not ...
do ya feel lucky punk?

Well, do ya???

High on a Limoncello Sea

The captain asked if I knew how to operate the ship.
Of course I didn't, but I said I did.
I figured because I was adept
at decoding the way the winds whisper,
I could steer the thing clear of icebergs and buildings.
And also, I was well versed
in the traditional Italian process
of making Limoncello, which isn't much
but it is something pleasant to think about
if for any reason the ship should start to sink.

We're all pirates on the high sea walking the plank.
Mid-summer dreams wrapped up in snow
trying to find the key to the ocean's bedroom
so we can sleep off the haze of dead days.

We're all vigilantes on parole,
just one step away from the hangman's noose,
as we mix up a new batch of Limoncello
to ease the snap of the waiting rope.

Professor Barfly

When the wet night curls its inky fingers
around the stiff glass nape of summer's neck,
there is a shattering of unseen things
that speak in unintelligible languages.

Broken glass strewn across the slippery floor,
and outside the worn and well-swung door
of a shark-toothed, seedy, second-hand bar
can no longer safely guide me home,
as I try to negotiate the twists and turns
on this same-old, strangely-familiar highway.

Stumbling into bed with a slurry flop, a tiggy bop
and a headache in full gear, revving its engine,
racing a hangover hell-bent to win,
I swear I'll never do that again ....
But there's always a shine and a silver lining:
and the best part of the whole thing is
the people you meet.

I remember this one barfly in particular.
We came to know him as Professor Barfly.
"Every day it can't sun. Some days it has to rain."
He would always say that when he had a bad day.
He taught me the virtue of living life
one bottle at a time.

This one night we were all loud
and working through it real good
and Professor Barfly started in about
his new theory on quantum physics.
In that moment it all made so much sense.
Not just quantum physics, but life in general.
I can't remember how long that feeling lasted
but it was important.

He gave me all his knowledge and intelligence

via electronic synaptic osmosis of the seventh kind.
I was infused with everything off-beat yet true:
I can tell a twin otter glide from a singularity
in any given sea or sky.
I can spot a giraffe shapeshifting to a flea
in a heartbeat or mind slap.

I've become so all-knowing
that I don't even know
what I don't know,
if you know what I mean....
but of course you don't,
because you're just a human and I ...
I am the new improved Professor Barfly II
So put that in your pipe and smoke it, dope!

Soup Du Jour?

You've heard it and I've heard it.
You've said it and I've said it.
But what lies beneath?
What's the deeper epiphany to be gained?
       Ok ... ok ...ok...
I promise this won't be too serious.
Alright, let's get all poetic and stuff.

One day, as the clock struck one,
I didn't hear it and you didn't hear it.
I said, 'what's that noise?'
You said, 'I think the clock struck one.'
I said 'Which one? Who? What?'
You said, 'It was long ago but not far away
and the body of the stricken is lying deep beneath.'
I asked, 'Is there some deeper epiphany to be discovered?'
I was getting serious ... too serious ... so serious
that I broke into a monster freestyle poem
and became an invisible thread swimming through it,
breaking bones of the words and tones of the grammar
in a mish mash of perfectly punctuated skeleton soup.

And then as the clock struck two I knew just what to do.
I had stashed many a beer can for days just like this.
You could easily see where this was going,
so you asked me to grab you one as well,
which was a bit out of character for you,
and that made it all the more thirst quenching for me.

So, I continued stirring the perfectly punctuated skeleton soup
to a smashing bone marrow turn,
smiling like a demented Cheshire cat,
knowing that first spoonful of soup
would burn the tongue something terrible.
Then I turned to you and asked in sweet, sweet misery,
"Soup Du Jour?"

The Merciless Years

Too many days and nights rode by
on stallions hell-bent on their own demise:
Throwing love to wolves to dine on lust.
Never looking past the dying flame.

I've spent too many weeks, months and years
rolling and unrolling infinite lifetimes.
Throwing the leftover soul scraps to those same wolves.

See their delight as they eye the prize!
See their jaws as they devour!
Hear the insatiable gnashing of teeth,
sounding like an incompetent supervisor's growl
or the greedy snarl of a heartless landlord.

And then there's the years, the merciless years,
that keep on marching by in a torn, rag-tag two-step
to a tune played in three-quarter time.
All marred by a pirate's tyranny
and the lunacy of faint yapping-off
in some distant dimensional reality of the third kind.

It's all so wrong, yet it feels so right.
It fits too loose as it squeezes tight.
A short-shot day turns to endless night.

∞∞∞∞

The stallions are done with their hunger games.
The wolves are angry and calling them names.
No more love, lust or leftover scraps.
Just fading growls and defeated yaps.

The days and nights are a dying flame.
The wolves say the stallions are to blame ...
and the merciless years just keep marching on
to the rag-tag echo of a worn out song.

Who Knew???

Nothing could have been more beside the point.
And to keep going on like that!
Belaboring is just not a good look.
It's a wearing quality.

He kept talking about almost dying several times,
but he had never really crept toward the abyss.
He had never truly carried the load.

It was one thing to always talk about the poems,
but another thing to always be with the poem.
When you're attached like that
the death thing doesn't even fire the fuse anymore.
Too bad he hadn't seen it yet.

Actually he was a decent scribbler.
But he was stuck in an ink-well of obscurity,
and non-plussed Rorschach blurs ...
He couldn't even make a proper inkblot.

He seemed to think he was a poet,
but he kept trying to shred wet papers
too waterlogged to ever be dried out,
to ever be read even once by others.
And he couldn't even memorize his own name,
let alone a 200-word poem.

So, he committed to the mad venture
of staring directly up into the light.
and started carrying glass jars in his back pockets.
He learned how to candle the night
and took sips of fire that taught balance
and cleansed the wounds on his ass
he got from the shards of glass
that punctured his flesh
when slipping and falling over his ego.
Sadly, he never did master the art of balance,

but eventually he smartened up
and put the glass jars in his front pockets.

That was a few years ago.

I heard just the other day
he's still picking glass out of his ass
but still can't pick a decent poem out of his head.

All his pens and ink-wells dried up,
so he switched horses in mid-stream,
bought a rad set of carving knives.
Now he spends every day sharpening them,
and slowly he's starting to get the point.

Who knew???

Kind of, Sort of, Maybe

I've been kind of dreaming lately.
In a poetic sense.
The words are just so free right now.
The screaming in the background doesn't even stop the flow.

I've been kind of reckless lately.
In a dismantled sense.
It's how I'm navigating my wilderness right now.
The force feeding of vitamins won't even curb the cause.

I've been sort of into it lately.
In a collaborative sense.
A million thoughts tumbling down.
Scrambling to immortalize them before they fade.

I've been sort of out of it lately.
In a Plutonian alien sense.
Watching the tube but not really seeing it.
Even the animations surpassing the real thing can't fix me up.

I've been kind of, sort of not really here lately.
In a ghostly semi-dead sense.
The edges of universes merging and uncoupling.
The images flickering on and off don't bother me anymore.

Maybe it's a kind of ... 'kind of' world.
Maybe it's a sort of ... 'sort of' world.
Maybe it's not a world at all.
Maybe it's just a holographic universe ... after all.

I wonder ...
kind of, sort of, maybe ....

The Strive

What do you do when the strive is gone?
When the reaching for a thing
doesn't even seem to invigorate anymore.
Not even the moon matters.
Only that space in between seems viable.
Only that feeling of "by the throat and worn" seems tangible.
Only that drudgery seems without waste and tension.

What do you do when you find yourself
neither interested nor disinterested?
When the turning of the crank feels like
it wouldn't be able to wind anyone up.
Not even a bored shipping clerk somewhere.
Only a big-assed summer snow squall of impossibility
seems slightly worthwhile.
Only an armless man waving a white flag
would stand a better chance.
Only a few rounds of electric shock therapy
would feel more refreshing comparably.

What to do … What to do.   I'll tell you what you do!
You hang the moon higher than it's ever hung before.
You take that space in between and wear out the worn,
and then you kick that big-assed summer snow squall
square in its ever-lovin' ass
and punt it to the armless man waving a white flag,
so he can drop it and yell with a rebel yell *"Never Surrender!"*.
Electric shock therapy for Billy Idol
to make him feel more alive, more relevant.

And then, my friend, you can wind yourself up,
turn that rusty-assed crank past the limit,
get back the full-on strive
and feel that old-time invigoration again.
That's what you do my friend …
That's what you do!!

Worry Not

When you think you can't take it anymore, worry not.
There is no happiness without pain.

An eye for acceptance is necessary.
If one will not accept,
remove that outlaw eye and worry not.
There will always be a spare pair of glasses
for the choosing.

When you're sailing
and you're stuck in static waters, worry not.
There will always be enough wind for later on ...
early on.

No need to weep for the crooked lines
that just can't get straightened out. Worry not.
Elastic emotions will always ease their crimp.

When you think the load you carry
is heavier than your compatriots, worry not.
The scales will always tip to even-out in the end.

When you think the ride is too expensive
and the pain too much, worry not.
It is possible to embrace the agony
without being hurt too much.

If you think the ride is free
and you're numb to it all, worry my friend.
It's impossible to hang onto the ecstasy
without ripping your heart apart.

And when you think you can't take it anymore, worry not.
Remember, there is no happiness without pain.

Gulls Circling

With the gulls circling high above,
men attempt to smooth the waters with flat irons,
and I wonder, rather conversely,
if it's time to become absorbed in the ripples.

I've noticed when fish swim the shallows for easy food,
the gulls circling high above circle lower,
in ever-diminishing circles, beak-bent to spear an unsuspecting fish,
and I wonder if fish are stupid, oblivious,
or simply couldn't give a gill.
Perhaps it's time to start more fish farms,
for fish safety's sake alone.

When circling lower to find its fish of choice
I've seen the sheer terror in a gull's eye,
when hungry dogs run the beach and wade and splash the waves,
and I wonder if the dogs really mean it
when they snarl and bark menacingly.
Perhaps its time to let them bond with the village parrot,
and feed them fish before we take them to the beach.

With the gulls circling high above
I pace in ever-diminishing circles far below,
and I wonder if the gulls take notice of me,
or if they're too absorbed in their screeching
and the expansive never-ending sky they fly in,
and I wonder if it's time to pepper that sky with lead,
to put an end to this predatory parade right here, right now.

I watch the gulls circling and I realize:
every gull knows beak-speak,
every fish has a tall tale,
every dog has his day,
each man walks the journey of his choice,
and every creature chooses ...
 according to his taste.

Covid, Impeachments, Insurrection and the Steal

I can see clearly now *(said in Johnny Nash voice):*
We all want some kind of completion, closure. Don't we?
Oh no, maybe not. That was then and this is now
and now, that's not the thing.
To be at home in the now, right now.
Now that's the thing ... yes it is!

In many senses, reality's been torn down last year.
And I've been shorn down to my last tear.
Now, that's not a bad thing.
Maybe it's what we all needed right now.
Species need a good shake up now and again.
I need a good shake up now and then.

Covid, impeachments, insurrection and the steal.
I still can't believe how odd these times feel.
It's a broken helicopter crashing to the ground.
It's a senator twisting his bobble-head around.
It's a fish out of water gasping for breath.
It's the Covid spectre of run-rampant death.

Confusion is my baseline ...
and I'm fine with it.

If you think it's ok ... drop the *"k"*
And put it in front of the "now", and then,
Maybe then, you'll *know* what I'm talking about!

Mebbee, Mebbee Not

Never one to follow a recipe,
I've concocted many throw away meals in my day
and stirred up too many sweet whiskey sours.
I've imbibed at all the run-down bars in town
and I've ate at all the greasy spoons around.

What I've found most interesting, through it all,
is that enlightenment always seems to shine brightest
in the dullest and most mundane of moments.
I mean, the balance is everywhere it isn't ... when it is,
until you blow a job you were counting on
or blow a tire in rush hour on a freeway bridge
or blow your ever-lovin' constantly reeling mind
and then the scales do an extreme limbo dance
that sees you trying to keep your balance
when the bar is two inches from the floor.

Impossible you say? Mebbee, Mebbee not.
I like to misspell 'Maybe' every chance I get.

After much time spent searching my muddled mind
in unrewarding, running in circles, introspection,
I turn the stove off and empty the ice bucket.
And I think of how, on every street,
sealed windows glow with orange cubes of firelight
like rectangular candle-wax Suns inside houses
built by displaced Black Forest architects.
And I think of how all those fake houses
resonate and resound with Cuckoo-clocks
that imitate the season of a perpetual spring.

It's the time of the season in a winter down summer.
Too cold and too hot at the same time. You do see that, right?
There's never gonna be a another red and gold autumn.
The whole year is stuck inside a belated spring.
You do see that too, right?
Anyhow, I'm getting hungry and thirsty

So I'm gonna triple toss and throw together
some super groovy, great, throw-away meals.
Then I'll mix up some, fresh from the vat,
super-sickly-sweet whiskey soursand then,
perhaps when my thirst is quenched,
I'll be able to dream into my own eyes
and see myself reflecting in yours.

Impossible you say? Mebbee, Mebbee not.
I like to misspell 'Maybe' every chance I get.

You do see that, right?

Ramble on Baby

All I ever wanted was to drink the finest of wines.
All I ever wanted was to eat the finest of meats and cheeses.
The good stuff just feels different.
It touches the palette and slips down the throat,
enters the stomach
and just arrives differently.

Inside my rickety, rag-tag, shaky house of cards,
I flick the old antique light switch to the up position
and the room becomes illuminated with old gold light.
I turn the new modern light switch dimmer knob
and the room is awash in new and improved light.
Or is it? Maybe it's just recycled lumen molecules
from a far and close parallel universe.

All I ever wanted was to be the finest me I could be.
All I ever wanted was to espouse the finest of words.
The intelligent stuff just feels different ...
Taller, wider, better, stronger and more empathetic.
It touches the heart and slips into the soul, enters the spirit
and just arrives differently.

I flick my mind on to super-sonic setting
and switch my thoughts to crazed attention.
My world shimmers and vibrates to a turn
and becomes a bright spinning, neon, strobe light.
I see the orchestra pit but there are no instruments.
No tablature, score sheets or conductor.
There's music playing, somewhere in the boonies,
but I can't see it. I can't hear it but I can feel it.
I turn the tuning knobs to high, higher, highest
and the bass controls to bing, bang, booming.

My room becomes a closet
filled with confetti and balloons.
In the corner stands a rubber high-boy mocking me,
and in a fragile paper mache dresser drawer

I am nestled tightly between my socks and underwear.
But the claustrophobia feels different ... almost comforting.
Or does it? Maybe it's just me
wearing heavy metal rose-coloured glasses
that were hewn from the sands of Mars just for me.
Yes... I think that's right.
They were from Mars for sure.

I feel like a broken record that won't stop skipping.
I'm becoming new and improved recycled light.
I'm moving into the far and close parallel universe.
Or am I? Maybe I've always been there.

Maybe ... 'maybe' is mebbee there
and mebbee I'm not really here at all.
Hark! I hear a voice encouraging me sweetly ...
Ramble on baby ... just ramble on.

The Big Shake Off

If you've ever been shaken off
    with a single shrug,
then I'm guessing you are nodding in agreement right now.
If you've ever fallen in love with a sound
so beautifully heavy you almost couldn't carry it, but you did.
Then I'm guessing you caught the general drift of the emotion;
and you're nodding in agreement right now too.

There are times when the universe is a big yawning void,
skulking, off-shoulder, and we just can't shake it off.
It's chasing you, just like it's chasing me
toward the edge of a jagged cliff called chance,
where you don't even get a chance to roll the dice.
It's the old sad story of mice and men and men and mice.
Buy the book, and read it once, then read it twice.
And then, if you learned anything from it,
shake it off with a double shrug. Shake a leg and walk away.

Sometimes you can just be walking along,
minding your own business; feeling the wind, seeing the stars.
Just being a part of the whole universe around you.
It feels so good for a moment ... until it doesn't.
So, you just shake it off with an off-hand shrug.

We've all been shaken off,
    but the trick is
to pick yourself up, dust yourself off
and get back in the game ... peel off the shame.
Find some poor unsuspecting hapless victim
who's in need a bit of a wake up; a bit of a shake-up.
Take the high road down to the low road. Speed it,
then shake him down and shake him off.

All it takes is a single hard-assed shrug ...
    And then it's done.

Shackles

Hope has its own shackles ...
Don't forget that.

The absurdity of ambition in a bunch of primates
on a floating rock makes me smile.
Pan Troglodytes aka chimpanzees share 98.7% of our DNA
They resemble us so little and yet we share so much.

The outcome of that which we live for
is no different than that which we die for.
We're hoodwinked and handcuffed to death and his brother
and we're desensitized and disoriented by life and its comrades.
Both willing partners in crime in a tug of war for our time.
Opponents, pistol-whipped on a tipsy chess board,
resembling an old-world, gangsta form of Russian roulette.

It all comes down to this:
The same price tag, according to the royalty fee.
The same background music, according to the beat; the rhythm.
The same choices we make, according to our state of mind.
The same steel bars, according to the way we temper them.
The same uniforms and faces, according to the way we fashion them.
The same ball and chain, according to our fears.

But, hope, hope has its own shackles ...
Don't ever forget that.

Clear Cut Corners

I've seen circumstances alter and falter,
but even then, dire circumstances or fair weather,
we stand in stoic elasticity. We remain the same.

The air is black these days with clear-cut corners
curling and winding through a rainforest jungle
piled mile-high with ice-cold sweat and cement tears.
Where the bizarre is commonplace and coveted
and sanity seems gentle and near yet still out of reach.

I coax my mind's magnifying lens from its cranial closet:
To get a better look at recent circumstances.
To understand why they alter and falter constantly.
There is no rest from this barrage of mostly unwelcome changes.
Even the good ones keep turning bad, upon close inspection.

One time I thought I saw myself in another dimension
becoming the favoured one's covered-up resurrection.
I was standing in the crack of a hazy clear-cut corner.
In the mirror of my mind I resembled Jack Horner
and my face was covered with half-devoured Christmas pie
and stuffed in my mouth was the plum
I'd pulled out with my thumb.
Then suddenly Thumbelina crashed my private party,
danced in on turf-stained graffiti-scarred golf shoes
and twirled to her death in a Christmas pie nightmare.

I live in my own private world of secrets and whispers:
Where melancholy keeps knocking on my door.
Where the bizarre is commonplace and coveted
and sanity seems gentle and near yet still so out of reach ...

The dark is filled with clear cut corners
and you're on the cheating side of town.
So when you're lightning the candle up,
you can burn one down for me.

That Damned Hole

I've noticed the hole gets a little deeper each year.
(that's right. The one I dug. Yeah, I'll take the credit).
And I stand above the hole all sturdy and indignan.
looking down into the abyss of my own creation.
Watching now change to then.
I probably should have noticed all of this earlier.
But I was too busy and bugged-up
with pushing well beyond myself.

Yes, I admit it. I've been too busy feeling the world.
Too busy watching the lemmings
run toward limestone cliffs and dead-end drops.

That damned hole. It just keeps getting deeper
and now it's filling with heavy dreams
gasping and drowning in heavy water.

Heavy, heavy hangs over my head.
I think I'm alive but feel I am dead.

There's always a prayer perched on my lips...
a prayer that refuses to fly through the ether
to the man who can answer and make it all right.
But he's probably been too busy and bugged-up
with all the pleas swimming in his spirit
all the voices pushing and shoving to be heard first.

He's a shoe-in for being too busy feeling the world.
Too busy watching the hapless humans
heading into the eye of the hadron collider
Too busy happily watching the planet slide of earth;
the world he built with such hope,
that spiralled into the depths of dread,
edging closer to an approaching black hole.
Sitting back in front of his big screen viewer
knowing all traces of his failure would soon be erased.

I too have been too busy watching the world
to concentrate on my own personal world of things.
Things detached and dangling on a wire.
Some sliding down a greased quarter line
and, on days like this, I think that's just fine.

I'm so tired of feeling the world crumbling to dust
and watching the unpracticed Evel Knievel lemmings
stunt buckle their failed canyon jumps between cliffs.

That damned hole. That damned hole!
It just keeps getting deeper and deeper
and now it's filling up with stale earth dust,
prematurely dead stunt lemmings,
and heavy, heavy water.

Heavy, heavy hangs over my head.
I think I'm alive but I'm sure I am dead.

The Big Questions

It's as crazy as Bukowski
not keeping any carbons of his works.
I mean, he just wrote it and sent it out, hoping for the best.
     Aren't we all just hoping for the best?
And what about Linda Lee? Wife and curator of his estate.
     Is she still shuffling through tear-stained poems?
     Or just collecting royalties from a dead guy.

It's as crazy as Maude
turning her eternal lights out on her 80th birthday.
I mean, she just woke up and blew out the candles
with a handful of pills and glass of room temperature water.
     Don't we all feel our own death when it's coming?
And what about Harold? Poor star-crossed, disturbed Harold.
     Why didn't he drive his car off that cliff when she died?
     Not heartbroken enough would be my guess.

It's as crazy as waiting for life to happen...
yet it's happening all the while.
I mean, we sit around longing and waiting and wanting
and pining for the things we already have.
     Why don't we know what we already have?

It's as crazy as tuna salad and Harvard beets in the morning
paired with Beaujolais wine and Beaudelaire madness.
I mean, doesn't it always make sense at the time?
Doesn't it always feel like an immortal poem?
     Aren't we all living immortal poems?

     In the end we're all masochists
     breaking our own hearts
     as we savour the flavour
     of becoming the flavour
     of our own heartbroken daze
     in the hazy maze of our days.

The Mystic

As Sunday afternoon begins to wind down,
I sit here chopping and playing with words.

I'm often asked why I write poems.
I usually respond by saying
'Someone has to tether the mystic's point of view
to the ever-changing human experience.'

They will then often ask if that means I'm a mystic.
I ask them, aren't we all?
Aren't we all unknowing poets?
Aren't we all speakers of wisdom if we choose to be?

And then they ask me what it means to be a mystic.
At this point I usually smile and simply ask them
if they ever spend their free time marveling at foolishness.
This is where we will often part ways.

Why? Because I love traveling through the Mystic.
I love marvelling at absurdity, silliness and foolishness.
I love speaking of wisdom from an inane juxtaposition.
I love being a mystic disguised as a poet, disguised as a human.
I love taking the sublime to the absolute '*nth*' of ridiculous,
and I love having fun all by myself in an empty house.
But most of all I love writing poems that just flow;
the ones that just come to me from the ether and buzz my mind.

As Sunday evening begins to creep in
I will sit here with my chopped and tweaked words
and toss them into the air of my mind, 52 pickup style,
and let the words fall where they may.
And God, the angels and the ether willing ...
they will channel the words through the mystic
and I will have an immortal poem to give to the world.

Wishes

What a pity.
I wish we would stop all the pointless seeking
when we've so obviously arrived already.

I wish we could be persuaded, or blessed with clarity,
just for a moment, to see it all so clearly
in Cinemascope and Panavision
on the big, bad screen of everyday life.

But wishing is for suckers
and I would much prefer to be labeled
a man content with gazing into the staring wing
of a butterfly that can't seem to straighten up and fly right.
Or a man that stares at goats for divine inspiration.
I'd rather be labeled those than a sucker.
Hell, I don't even mind being labeled a mucker.

So now I will digress
into a digestible series of synaptic emissions:

If wishes were crack houses,
addicts would scream and dream away the crave.
Jelly Roll Morton's jazz would keep them dreaming awake
inside many crystallized mountains of snow.

If wishes were warm and cozy sanitariums,
alcoholics would withdraw and throw off the shakes.
Jerry Lee's music would rattle and roll
into every nook and cranny in their tortured soul.

But wishing is for suckers.
Lotteries are for losers,
and Horseshoes?
Well, that's anybody's guess ...
Personally, I don't give a toss.

The Quantum Matrix of My Mind

I'm a pulsating, abstract gravity well
that an unempathetic black hole created in space time
and then spilled me over into earth time and my time.
I'm deeply rooted in the quantum matrix of my mind
and all that firepower may not have been enough.
Maybe no amount of energy can shift my gears.
Maybe no amount of wind can dry my tears.
Maybe no amount of days can fill my years.

But ages and pages and stages
They beckon to me still in a low sultry voice.
My pen has grown legs and is walking toward me;
now it's broken into a sprint, trot, and finally a gallop.
Nearing the high jump it catapults into my hand
and lands deftly between forefinger and thumb.
They tighten like a mechanical vise around its casing.

I see my pen has brought along Hop-a-Long Cassidy.
Hoppy is doing a deranged one-legged dance
to the tune of a digeridoo played by Hop-Sing
who somehow ended up in the wrong cowboy tv show.
Through no fault of the producers, I might add,
but perhaps I won't. There's too many disclaimers already
in this twilight zone, crazy, mixed-up shit show.

And on another note, Ben Cartwright is really pissed,
He and the boys having to cook their own meals.
The cooking is substandard and super tasteless
and Hoss is barely recognizable these days.
Forced onto the absentee Hop-Sing diet,
he's now just a wisp of a man.
A mere shadow of himself.

They're all just a bunch of carbonized silicone puppets.
Displaced, disoriented and disillusioned in fantasyland.
They're pushing, and grabbing at crimps and chips
as they frantically look for footholds and handholds

trying to grasp them with lobster claw hands and feet,.
to climb out of this pulsating, abstract gravity well I am.
This unempathetic black hole created in spacetime.

Once I can successfully reclaim *my* time
and uproot myself from the quantum matrix of my mind,
I'll buy a free ticket to ride and run for Congress.
I'll campaign with my pages on podiums and stages
and promise to right all the wrongs of these ages.

I'm a sure-fire bet to get elected no doubt,
because I can make silk poetry out of a sow's ear.
and I can make onion-skin paper out of eagle feathers
and ink out of blood, sweat and bone.

My rhetoric will be thunderous, a sky tsunami,
and my lightning quick wit will be fierce and fast.
I'll baffle my opponents with refried bullshit
and reel in my voters with my unbreakable line of promises
attached to my rock-solid rod of honesty.

I'mma gonna be the best damn elected official
ever created in spacetime, earth time or my time:
And no amount of bad vibes can unstring my guitar.
And no amount of negative media can rain on my parade
And no amount of warped track can stop my train.

Hold on tight you Washington muckers.
Look out man! I'm comin' for you!!

Freefall

One more step. Don't look down,
I tell myself reassuringly.
I'm stepping off the ledge and freefalling
through my kaleidoscope dreams of neon and ice.
Becoming a part of the me I've never met.
The me that loves to climb to the diamond apex of sky
and fall from the dizzying heights in a calypso heartbeat
to a land filled with sighs and songs and poetry.

Falling into my dream of my former self
I see an old baseball bat, Barbie and Ken dolls and a slinky toy
standing on the steps to eternal childhood.
Where magnifying-glass fried ants lay stone-dead
on concrete driveways laid bare under a torrid July sun;
and ancient goldfish swim in a man-made murky pond
that's never been filtered or cleaned since it was made.
There's only one goldfish left now, and it isn't gold anymore.
And there's only one me left now, and it isn't me anymore.

As the freefall ends, I alight with sure-footed grace
onto the black and green checkerboard plexi-glass
of rippling water on the glazed boardwalk below,
where all that's left are two choices: walk or swim.

But what if you were born to fly? What then?
I guess the only consolation would be water-wings.
If the dream is water and you are the air
and there is no solid ground to be found anywhere
then I guess you'll have to sink or swim.
Flying was never a choice.
So we may be forced to succumb to the paradox ...
a bit confounded and weariness tinged.

There are limits to reason, aren't there?
Can we ever truly come to a mutual agreement
among ourselves? I mean ever?
Wherever does this wildly ignorant pursuit

for control and meaning even come from?
Alright, alright.
Enough of that.
Back to flying.
The sky does offer such a peaceful
and unyielding embrace.
And the cloudscapes.
Oh, the majestically empty cloudscapes.

As it turns out this is where it all began.
The collaboration days turned to years in these clouds.
Rising seemingly out of nowhere.
But they were always there.
Patient. Omnificent. Omniscient.
Just waiting for us to fly.

And now ...
we've given each other wings.

Run Boy Run

I couldn't run out of that room fast enough.
She just stayed near the window,
staring out into the floating valley
that seemed to be moving all night.

When we first got there
she asked me if I always do what feels right.
I remember thinking to myself,
what an odd question to ask someone
as they are about to rap on a door.

I told her nothing had felt right
since she turned off the moonlight
so as not to see her night shadow anymore.
She always did say she shone her brightest
at the nadir of midnight.

We stood there in silence after rapping.
The door creaked open of its own accord. Nobody in sight.

We entered and sat at a glass blown table that made no sense.
Its structure was all wrong and, to boot, it couldn't talk
in any kind of coherent sentences or even fragmented phrases.
It was an inane dangling modifier glued to the floor boards
modifying absolutely nothing of consequence.

We sat in our electric chairs
waiting for the warden of the séance.
Seconds to minutes to hours. We didn't talk.
We were uncomfortable.

When we were almost falling asleep
in the clutch of total boredom.
an ear-splitting, atmosphere-shattering scream
erupted from above and a grotesque figure
began descending into the gloom.

Our speech had been snatched from us
like a dead rabbit from a hat.
I looked at her. She was shining bright and smiling
an otherworldly sinister grin
that burst into blood curdling cackling laughter.

I kicked myself out of my electric chair
and ran at breakneck speed,
crashing through the door now turned to confetti.
I couldn't get out of that cursed room fast enough.

I don't know what happened to her
but sometimes, staring out into the floating valley
that seems to be moving at night ...
sometimes I swear I see her shining.
I can still hear here cackling laughter
and I shudder ... I mean really shudder,
and I can't get out of the room fast enough.

The Bliss

The bliss is out there somewhere.
It must be.
Or maybe it's in here somewhere.
It could be.
Finding it is probably like doing a thing without thinking.
I was never any good at not thinking though.
But I do somehow finally feel like I'm on the cusp.
Of what I don't know.
But I know I'm close.

I've been far past the edge looking for it
and still never found it.
I've become the craziest of the breed looking for it
and still never found it.
I've stared directly into the eyes of days
and mind-melded with the dark of night
and still I never found it.
And then one day I just stopped looking. Stopped striving.
That's when I noticed the faintest of flutters
in that space of the soul I'm rarely able to access.
I saw the two sides of it all: It's really a 2D universe.
The yin and the yang; differences married to each other:

      the body kiss, the soul bliss.
      the body bliss, the soul kiss.

And now I peer out from inside myself with new eyes,
and new understanding glowing and growing.

If you look too hard for something, you'll usually overlook it
and if you stop looking for it and it is meant for you,
it will find you.

All things come to pass then come to pass again,
as time turns inside out and burns
a fiery kiss into immortal bliss.

Feelin' It and Knowin' It

The problem is this.
Speaking in tongues only doesn't make sense
to those not speaking it.

The power behind the words and sounds is evident.
But people don't listen to the power.
They want it to make sense to them.

Bob Marley said "He who feels it, knows it."
Like I said, the power is what we feel.
The words are what we hear.

It's like whiskey.
Whiskey when you're sick makes you well.
Whiskey makes you sick when you're well.
Whiskey's a relief to some and poison to others.
Heavy metal music to one seems so cool.
The same sound to other ears comes off as cruel.

Same thing rings true with power.
When wielded by a saint it's benevolent.
When wielded by a demon it's destructive.

So many words are lost in translation.
So many feelings beyond explanation.
Like the word 'love'. To some it means 'like'.
To some it means 'lust', and to some it means 'caring'.
It is a powerful word filled with different emotion.

Take the word 'and'. Nothing powerful about it.
Never will be. It's just a peon on the language social scale.

The power of words is nothing to be trifled with my friend,
and that is why I speak in tongues.
Speaking in tongues is what sets us apart
from the understated un-understandable majority.

We, the minority, don't want to be understood by the masses.
We just want to be understood by them that's like us ...
and damn the few who speak with forked tongues.
Yeah you heard me right. "Damn the few."

Now I'm growing weary. My tongue needs some medicine.
Imma gonna pour me 3 fingers of home-brew whiskey,
and Imma gonna turn up my grunge-metal CD.
And then Imma gonna sing along in garage-band tongues ...

But hark! I hear a tap-tap-tapping on my door,
and I know it's not a lost woodpecker.

I shuffle-step out of my lazy-boy,
dance a cool new groove to the music,
then side-step through levitated hula hoops to the door,
and throw it open in wide-eyed surprise!

....For God's sake...can you believe it?
It's Bob Marley sayin' hello buddy in tongues.
And we're both feelin' it and knowin' it.
Bob's just a shufflin' on in and feelin' the power:
Yeah man! Just feelin' it and knowin' it
like he's never known feelin' it before.

We high five each other and wink our crossed eyes.
I pour us a triple alcoholic bullet.
We lift up our glasses in solemn salute,
and yell out the long-livin' desperado chant ...

Let's hoist to the dark types.
Let's drink to the archetypes,
To the Freuds and the Jungs.
Let's hear it for the tongues!

Yeah man!
Let's hear it for the tongues!!!

The Numbers of Timeless Time

Rubber souls and retrograde bars,
lost black holes and renegade stars
are all that's left to fill up the empty.
Beer bottle dreams torn apart at the seams,
yesterday's heroes in apron string themes
can't make any sense of this world of clouds.

These kind of things cattle prod my thoughts
and parade out of step through my questing mind.
These goddamned trivialities.
Compounding my disinterest.
Confounding all my failed insurrections.

And I think there is a better way to deal with life.
I think those pesky candy-stripers have got it all figured out,
and it's so good they're all getting face-lifts
and fitness-memberships to keep body toned and arabesque.
But that gets old pretty quick when you're young and pretty,
so they just spend years and years playing marbles for fun
until they finally lose all theirs to the boogey-man ... dememtia.

Everything comes down to numbers...EVERYTHING!!!
5,6,7,4,=22 minus 33 = -11 in double zeronomics;
and that's the true equation.
Pick up sticks, deal the cards and throw the dice
7, 5, 9 and 56 =77 divided by 7 = +10 in decinomics;
and that's the quantum root liaison.
The right and the left. The bass treble clef.
Both end at the same end of the never-ending circle.

I know these mind-boggling super intelligent things
because I'm well versed in the mathematics of poetry
and even more adept in the poetry of mathematics.
They're interchangeable you know. Yep they sure are..
It's the algebra of words and the geometry of grammar
that have to fit exactly to square the Pi in the Rs-hole.
It's all really just a crackerjack box without a prize.

The story of my sorry-ass life most days.
A can of bully beef in the black hole of your eye
where cantankerous aliens keep trying on shoes that don't fit.
What a shit show watching them slip, stumble and fall.

I see out of the corner of my eye
the candy stripers have returned to the scene
and are going barefoot in the restaurant.
I think that's a health infraction
but I'm not sure if its an algebraic in-fraction
or a geometric fulcrum of traction in-fraction.

Either way, no matter what you do or see or play,
everything vibrates to numbers.
Everything is mathematics
and there really are only 2 numbers:
Zero and one in a trillion zillion combinations
spinning like binary orbs around each other
trying to compute the equation to end all equations.

And now, when it's too late,
all the rubber souls
have been swallowed by the lost black holes
and the retrograde planets
have been burnt to ash in the renegade stars,
and there's nobody left to fill up the bars.

Beer bottle dreams are now nightmarish themes
and all of our haphazard lives
have just been a random experiment in time.
Just an experiment
in the numbers of timeless time.

A Glorious Nonsense
aka Sanostat in Evidaris

I'm pretty sure today is a Tuesday.
In February.
What a glorious nonsense.
The naming of days and months.
And seconds and minutes and hours for that matter.
Next, you're going to tell me they even have a name
for those fireworks in the sky.
I bet you're going to say they call them stars.

You can keep your names.
I prefer to engage with the mysterious ways of it all,
as I spin around myself like a bottomless top.

It's like they want to put their iron hands in velvet gloves,
and their second hands on numbered faces
named wristwatches and clocks.
They even give them family names ...
Grandfather clocks and Grandmother clocks, and on and on.
What sense does that make?
Why is everyone so concerned with the external?
Categorizing it, pigeon-holing it, naming it.

Look, I know what you're thinking.
Does it always have to be soooo serious?
It's a fair question.
Let me put it this way;
I stay on point when it's time to be serious.
and I get loose when it's time to be frivolous.
I just try to nonchalantly fit into your glorious nonsense.
To be honest, it's like its own spontaneous manifestation
of the ridiculous giving birth to the sublime.

I'd like to think I have little to do with anything.
And everything to do with the rest.
Which, in truth, is the truth.
It's such a glorious nonsense

this madness you all absorb yourself in.
But, what do I know?
I'm just a visiting binary being
from an, as yet, undiscovered star system
who has become too at home here.

Spinning myself around like a bottomless top
I sing this naming world holographic
that I may see it and walk through it untouched.

Where I hail from....see I'm too comfortable here
even unconsciously using your colloquialisms.
Drop that thought.

So now, today,
totally into my comfort zone here,
I'm wondering what we would call this day back home,
if we imbibed in such glorious nonsense
as the naming of intangibles.

I'm pretty sure we'd name today Sanostat.
In Evidaris.

The Power Behind These Moments

Can we take a moment
to speak on dangerous happenings
like falling in love?
Or allowing the walls to come down?
Or mystical experiences?
There is a power behind these moments.

When something like falling in love happens:
It's as if all the luck comes at once.
It's as if the dealer slides you a couple of aces under the table.
It's like being on the space shuttle when it explodes
and you're the only survivor ... and, no injuries either.
It's like you're swimming with sharks and they like you so much
they've taken the time to teach you their language
and also invited you to the shivers' next extravaganza wedding.
Yeah, then you know you're the lucky one ... the chosen one.

And, when the walls come down and the spirit flies
through the mystical ether of soul:
It's like being Joshua in Jericho when the walls tumbled down.
It's like being a novice turned genius at Eckankar soul travelling.
It's like being Eckhart Tolle in a candy-apple red corvette
skirting a huge border line-up and guards by levitating over the que
and finding solace in the arms of the angels for a second or two.
It's like being born breathing and dying breathless all at once.
AND ... thoroughly enjoying it all over and over again.

When this kind of stuff happens to you:
You know you are deep inside the power of the moment.
You know you're the lucky one ... the chosen one.
You know you are the mystical experience,
the power behind the moment,
forever cast *in living technicolour.*

Yes Indeedie!

What would it feel like to be one in spirit with the universe?
Would it feel like an astounding paradox?
Would it feel like that strange magical place
where every once in a blue diamond moon
you can get even beyond the poetry
and into the glove of the oneness?

Would it feel like one hell of a waste of words
to even attempt to explain it?

It's a bit of a miracle and a tad of a quandry
but don't worry about all these things.

When you are one with the universe
you will become the true essence of strange magic
and you will be so far beyond the poetry
it will be a new form of communication
and you will be part of the soft supple skin
inside the glove of oneness with the universe.

When you become one with the universe
you can just sit back and doobie-ize *the everything*
and you will know why the nothingness is so empty.
Then you'll discover, with amazing alacrity,
the tension and alien fabric of the strings
dictating the many splendiferous movements
of the puppets we are becoming and unbecoming.
with the urgent inconstancy of windblown forest fire.

Yes indeedie!
When you become one with the universe
it will be one mother of a hallelujah,
a rejoicing of birth and death ad perpetuum
and all the flavours, tastes, aromas and emotions savoured
in the eye-popping clip of each astounding paradox.

Long Gone

As the sun shines.
As the rain falls.
Like every pure smile singing that night.
As the moments move.
As the hearts awaken.
Like every soft touch that missed that night.

There's a heartache behind every smile
as time suspends the emotive self
and hypnotizes the spirit into woken slumber.
As every vengeful pencil connects the dots of desperation
that lead to the hole in my heart that I hide from the world.

I've been travelling these twists and turns too long.
They feel so familiar and easy now. No surprises anymore.
Like the night that rolls in darker with every curve.
As the mountains in the distance yawn and disappear.
As the river so far below beckons and calls.
Like every suicide curve I once chose to negotiate.

As the wheels whine and the track clicks
and that lonesome whistle calls
I reach for the throttle and push it full thrust,
one last time.

The smiles and the singing
are now only a distant memory.
As the sun shines.
As the rain falls.
As the wheels whine
As the whistle calls.

I'm here and yet I'm long gone.

Stray Dogs

Sometimes the sun shines brightest on the stray dog.
And sometimes the branch breaks
underneath the weight of the lightest squirrel.
Who's to say this isn't fair?
Who's to say this isn't the way it's supposed to be?

Sometimes the ugly duckling becomes a prom queen.
And sometimes the boy, who used to bottle his despair
and offer it to anyone in need, wins the nicest smile superlative.
Who's to say the underdog has to lack confidence?
Who's to say the good, the bad and the ugly can't change places?

A bit more here about the stray dog
who may just be an avatar for the lost human.
Maybe he was just minding his own business,
on his daily morning walk through the park,
when he stopped to take a piss on an old oak tree,
and in the middle of this bodily function
he didn't hear the branch above him cracking and breaking,
under the weight of the anorexic squirrel dancing on it.
Branch down. Squirrel safe. Dog coldcocked.

It was a random knockout blow to Bow-Wow's head.
No even a yip or a yelp or a whimper. Just out!
When he woke up he didn't recognize the park,
didn't know who he was, where he was,
or even which direction his home was ...
if, in fact, he even had a home.
Who's to say this is fair?
Who's to say this is the way it's supposed to be?

And what about all the manuscripts ever written in the dark
that never saw the light of day or a publisher's good side.
Maybe they just weren't in the right place at the right time,
being viewed by the right person with the right attitude.
Sometimes a great manuscript sits on the shredding dock:
all those hours of sweat and toil marked for destruction ...

almost like the words weren't important, like they never counted.
Who's to say which writing is strong enough to stand on its own.
Who's to say which pearls of wisdom just aren't good enough.

And what about all those frustrated poets
who never get their poems published, read or even heard.
What about them ... the repressed underappreciated majority?
Maybe they were just too channeled from beyond
to ever really get a firm foothold in the here and now.
Maybe they were too busy moving in and out of the ether
to ever stay in one place long enough to buy stamps,
or get online or into cyberspace.
Who's to say that writer wasn't earmarked for fame.
Who's to say that poet wasn't positioned for greatness.

So next time you see a homeless down and outer,
maybe it's through no fault of his own.
Maybe it's the fault of those dancing squirrels
who crapped all over him.
Maybe he can't remember the good times
buried so far underneath all the branches piled on him.
Who's to say he's just a victim of circumstance.
Who's to say he would have ended up here anyway.

Sometimes the sun shines brightest on the stray dog
and sometimes it just hides behind a cloudy sky.
So the next time you see a poet
reciting passionately to no one and the stars
Just remember this:
We're all stray dogs, aren't we?
Searching for that part of us we can truly call home.
Waiting for our shine in the sun.

Monochromatic Calico

On the eve of the morning on the cusp of yesterday,
on the 6th day after the 7th and sundown before twilight,
I'll be riding high in a calico sky,
on a cumulus cloud of thoroughbred horses,
racing against the metronomes of time
and dreaming of daisy chains and 4 leaf clovers.

It's upon these horse clouds,
I will summon all the things I know not of.
It's also here that I would tell you,
the sky itself would cry if I ever let you down.
Don't forget that.

On the eve of the evening
that shall usher in eternity,
this day will seem just like
the 1st day after the 2nd big bang.

I'll be embracing you
like the lost warmth of summer
and we will be riding together,
high in a sky no longer calico,
but rather monochromatic,
deriving from a single base hue
and extending using its tints.
And tones.
And shades.
Glowing in its oneness.
On the cusp of our tomorrow.

The Speaking Universe

The behavior of the winds,
like the dancing flames in a fireplace,
can be far more genuine
than even the greatest speakers of wisdom.

The wobbly hesitation of so many lost souls,
just like the chicken's beak to the chalk line
can't help but put a finger out,
in vain attempts to touch the moon.

The hard-held belief that the sun is boiling
could be the greatest fallacy ever espoused,
but then again it could be true, probably is true.
But what of our limited knowledge of temperatures.
I mean we keep changing the methods,
by which we measure the size and weight of things.
Hell, we keep changing the scales of measure
for everyone and everything:
Linear to decimal. Fahrenheit to Celsius.
Miles to kilometers, Quarts to liters. Etc. etc. etc.
Do we really know the true measurement of anything?
Methinks not. Methinks Cold. Methinks hot.
But nothing is cold and nothing is hot
It's all intangible and only a thought.

And inebriation. So many wildly different measurements
to ascertain if the drinker is over the legal alcohol level.
If he walks the line heel to toe and doesn't falter
then he's deemed sober enough. And again keeper of the keys.
But, he could just be a very practiced equilibriumist,
practicing on his backyard white line for times like this.
Or he could just be one lucky shmuckarooni!
If he doesn't walk the line, then the second measurement ensues.
Breathing into a plastic tube so his breath can be analyzed
Give me a break. He could have just ingested a whack of cough syrup
and the reading may be a false positive... So go figure.
So I say measurements are...wait for it ... shit!

I've done time in the prison of wobbly indecision,
and skinned my ass holding my nose to the grindstone.
But I still believe the moon is only a fingerprint away
and the sun is a con-artist iceberg in full disguise.

I know fire needs air to ignite
and flames love to dance in the catch of her breath.
And I know the greatest speakers of wisdom
are just an ember in the fire, a speck in the flame
and can't ever hold a candle
to the winds of the speaking universe.

Looking Back

Getting into the getting out of things ... a bit of a slippery slope.
Sometimes requiring Arnold Palmer golf cleat shoes.
Sometimes a rotating soft kayak fiberglass swim
to the least threatening side of the channel.
And then, just when you're almost out of it all,
that haunting little doubt that niggles at your mind...
Did I really want out? I mean really, really want out??

God, I hate second guessing myself, but you'd never know it
because I do it all the time... well most of the time.
Just like a double-check every night on the double check,
then I can't recall if I did double check, so I check again.
Then that blossoms into more second guessing.
I have to make sure the doors and windows are locked ... yet again
Yeah, I know I'm 6 floors up, but a super fit gymnast killer
could spider-man his way up to *moi* residence.
A chance I cannot take. There's more poems to write.

I realized a while ago that I'm past my best before date,
So now I'm in the middle of downsizing for death,
packaging and regifting gifts I received that I don't like,
to give to people I don't much care about for Christmas goodwill.
I don't think they'll know if they may have been used before.
But if they ask me, I'll just say, oh no, they're new.
I got them at a liquidation world clearance sale earlier this year.
So what are they going to do? Call me a liar? I don't *think* so.

Now I'm faced with the fact that I may live way longer than I think.
What do I do then, you may ask ...when I've gotten out of *things*
and there are no things left to occupy my days or nights?
No worries at all. I'll still have my poems to write,
and alas, they'll never all be done even when I'm all done.
Looking back, I sigh, and wonder why I titled all my poems,
when they should have been able to speak for themselves.
Ahhhh ... sweet mystery of life ... I realilze now they do.
But most people just don't hear.

Mind Stylus

I've seen a lot of paintings that were substandard.
I've seen a lot of sculptures that are ridiculous,
and I've read a whack of poems that just don't cut it,
can't even slice it or make the grade.

I know a good poem when I see one,
just like a shill knows a good mark when he sees one.

In a way, writing a poem is like betting on cards.
You have to know when to hold or fold.
When to grip the pen or lay it down.

The only difference is:
With a poem there's no bluffing.
It's got to be the real thing. T
he whole ball of wax.
There just ain't no getting' away from it.
Twisted Sister knew it, but couldn't do it,
so switched horses in mid-stream
and opted for the lesser life ...
the life of fame.

We poets don't want that. We don't seek fame.
What we want is true appreciation for the words.
The words we pull out of our grey matter and the ether.
We don't give a crap about making money at it.
We just want to make the words come together and work.

I actually feel sorry for the non-poets.
They'll never be able to see black as white,
and paint words with the stylus of their minds.
Why? Because they don't have a mind stylus.
Only true poets are blessed with that.

Trust me, I'm just fine here in my own lane.
It's here that the words push me to the edge
But haven't quite pushed me off the ledge.
Not yet anyway.

It's here that I grow with hunger.
It's from here I can see the beautiful sunrises
over Belfast Harbor.
It's here you can feel free to ask me anything,
as many times as you would like.
But I ain't giving up the tricks.

And it's here I can really see
the world turned upside down.
What a view!

So yeah,
I've seen a lot of lackluster things in my days.
But it doesn't affect me none.
It has just made me double my efforts
and try even less.

Beguiled yet?
See the mind stylus yet?
Grown past regret yet?
Yeah, I bet.

Let me leave you with this ...
There is no knowing
without a knower to notice.
You know?

Perhaps you do,
but, sadly, I'll bet you don't.

Cycles

I recently read somewhere, that some 150,000 people
die every day around the world.
I know very few of them; if any at all.
And also, just about that many, if not more,
are born every day around the world.

What does this mean you may ask?.
Nothing really. It's just another cycle.
It's all cycles really.
When I say "all" I mean everything.
From the micro to the macro.
It's all cycles.

I recently read somewhere that the shape of a circle
represents completion and fulfillment
in many cultures around the world.
I can't draw a perfect circle without a stencil.
Very few people can.
And also, the shape of a square
can be a house or a really boring person.

What does this mean you may ask?
Nothing really.
I can actually draw perfect circles.
Not physically.
I'm talking mental and spiritual
geometric geography; surreal orbs
drawn with the bicycle wheels of my mind.

They are perfect circles
shining splendidly in synchronous cycles of me.
It's all cycles really ...
It's all cycles.

Embrace the Emptiness

The emptiness falls through the streets,
creeps through the alleys, scales the wall,
climbs through my window and embraces me,
finds a vacant thought, mind drifting,
and takes up residence in my dream.

It's a lonely night's dream
and a dreamy night's loneliness.
The language is indecipherable; the images are hazy
like hieroglyphics of the mind becoming bizarre reality.

The sounds are cacophonic then muted in repetition.
The beat harsh, then indistinct, muffled
like cards dropped on slotted gunpowder then lush carpet.
Dog-eared cards, corner-cut, unshuffled, undealt,
falling like tiny cardboard houses, collapsing,
in slow motion retrograde film clip noire.
Exposing hidden closets harboring dark secrets.

In the distance a hollow bell rings out
inside the silent echo of a stolen midnight revelation.
I followed the sound of the bell until it fell silent.
There, in that spot where the bell stopped ringing,
I found there's a completeness to incompleteness.

So if we aren't missing anything why do we feel that way?
Go off in some spiritual direction if you must
but I had no choice.
What, was I going to do? Dismiss the calling?
Was I going to play dumb to the galvanization of the search?

There is something happening here.
Rest assured. You can take that to the bank.
But don't try to cash the check
I wrote you the other day.
Not yet anyway.
I may have spent some of that money

on the over-ripe, stale goodness
of an amateur fortune teller's vapid omniscience.
I simply asked her
           'When will I finally get there?'
To which she simply replied
           'You've already arrived.'

        So yes,
I've decided to embrace the emptiness,
and make love to the loneliness.

Feel free to join me
in this noble quest for enlightenment.

But you must let yourself in completely.

I insist upon very little,
but I do insist upon that.

We Are Not in Babylon

People who claim to be complicated, usually aren't
and people who claim to have hit rock bottom, usually haven't.

Complicated people don't have the time
to talk about their complicatedness
because they're too busy being complicated.
And people who survived rock bottom
would rather not re-live the experience,
by babbling on about it.
I know a guy who always yaps on and on about these things.
Complicated, rock bottom. Things he thinks he is, but isn't
We call him Babylon.

A wise man once said, *Don't talk about it. Be about it.*
Sage advice sure, but what about poets you ask.
Don't we often write of our complicated genius
and our regular visits to the dark places of life?
The bottomless rock bottoms only we know?
Yes. We do. And when we do, we really do it.
On paper, through microphones, at podiums and in books.
But if you ever meet me there's a good chance
you won't hear me spew or blurb about any of those things.
I save them for the paper.
And I save them for the pen.
No, my friend, if you hope to spend a day with me,
pounding back pints and wallowing ever so languidly
in *whatevers* and I've been *everywhere,*
you are bound to be deeply disappointed.

Don't get me wrong, we will drink plenty on that fine day.
But there will also be a lot of singing and laughing,
and maybe even some humbling, fumbling and stumbling.
It's not really complicated and this ain't rock bottom.
There's no pity pots to piss in here,
and definitely no pity parties here, mate ...
We are not in Babylon.

Samadhi Goals

I couldn't get the damn lid off the jar.
And to make it worse I couldn't find
my *old person,* jar gripper thing for the life of me.
All I wanted was some relish to add to the mayonnaise.
Was that asking too much?
I mean what's the point of tarter sauce without the relish?
That would be like skipping meals,
in an attempt to gain weight.
Or gluttonously roaming all you can eat buffets,
in an attempt to lose some poundage,

So I gave up on the culinary condiment endeavor
and decided to eat the fish sans sauce.
But before I could even take a bite
the thing looked up at me and said,
"You know there's another level to the whole thing.
You just haven't found it yet."

How odd I thought.
Not that the fish was talking to me,
but that I wasn't aware of the fact
I still had work to do on my levels.

I thought I had reached Samadhi this whole time.
Or at the very least I thought I was:
Just a couple of meditations away from
a mystical concentrating of mind
into an enlightened, calm, abiding poem.
Just a couple of decent sessions away from
levitation, spoon bending and astral travel.

Imma think Imma gonna start a brand new chop
for all the wayfaring questing questors
on and off planet Earth.
Imma gonna call it "A Jose Journey".
That's my new Samadhi Goal.

Hell I may even start a new movement.
A new and improved unreligious religion ...
JOSISM ... and the motto will be

> *How to find your way through the dark*
> *with a thermos of hot Darjeeling tea*
> *and a Taclight that can't do the job.*

All you need is faith brother.
Just a little faith.

That's really all we are:
      F.A.I.T.H.
Fiercely Ambivalent Inspired Talking Heads
just strivin' it man,
strivin' it to reach our Samadhi goals.

Right There for the Taking

We had gotten to a place
where we had no points of reference
except each other.

Not a bad place per se.
Simply a complication.
She's one of the things
that's made the trip enjoyable.
It's not that at all.
It's just that we had become one.
And the only question left was, "what now?"

There's a primal simplicity available for all interested.
You. Me. Any of us.
Seriously, it's right there for the taking.
That is to say, if you're not the type
to lose your nerve or lose your head.
Or if you're not the type
to act all illusory like a hypnotist.

There's really no distinction
between trying and not trying.
It's the same energy.
The process reveals itself:
To some early on.
To some late.
To some never at all.

There are so many things right there for the taking:
The air we breathe and the grass we walk on.
The sandy beaches and the oceans we swim in.
The light from the moon that shines in our eyes.
The stars we wish on and Jupiter and Mars.
But that's never enough for the elite,
the privileged, the politicians or the celebrities.
They are the much wants more creed of folks.

I decided to take a little trip down memory lane
so I time travelled back to the 50s.
I overheard a conversation,
in a closed restaurant on Broadway.

"I've got a plan," Frank said to Ava,
"First we take Manhattan and then,
we take what is, and has always been,
right there for the taking."

Then they sashayed away
singing goodbye to *New York, New York*
as they headed to:
The Union stockyards.
The Wrigley Building,
The razzamatazz and all that jazz
right there for the taking ...
in the one town that won't let you down.
Need I say it?
Perhaps not, but I will anyhow.
Chicago! *Their Kind of Town ...*

These Words

These words ... these word shuffle like cards,
then spill from the quiet volcanoes of my mind,
as I sit at my work desk pondering
why working is a thing we do.
But the mortgage lender is happy to remind me
why I work.
And my kid's love of fast food reminds me
why I work.

Everyday it's shit, shower and shave
then head to the drudge and leave my man cave.
Too much month at the end of the money.
That's why we work ... to make things work.

Another day, another penny and more of not any.
Today I'm going to splurge and take a taxi to Nirvana
and start a quest to round up all the missing words,
that wait oh so patiently to be found, written and heard.

Mortgage costs, bills, expenses, work ...
those words we don't like to hear or see
But these words, these words
don't know anything about work.

Maybe I can get off the work chain
and be a poem someday,
and relax in the exhilarating
and comforting company of
These Words,

Puzzling

I've been puzzling on an impossible jigsaw puzzle.
There are quite a few pieces missing and some broken.
The box it came in is long-gone and destroyed,
but I still have one pesky little piece of cardboard
stuck between my two front teeth.
Makes smiling a substantial chore.
I have to do it fast – flash open / flash closed,
like a camera speed shutter on crystal meth.

There are so many things I can't figure out.
So many impossible intangibles I live with.
Like constantly mind searching for the lost puzzle box
and brushing my teeth too much
trying to dissolve that god-awful piece
of mashed-up, saliva thrashed cardboard
that just won't leave its metal dental heaven
in the shiny enamel atmosphere of *my mouth.*
And now my tooth-brush is broken,
my thoughts are totally hammered
and coming unscrewed in scrapings,
And some new jig-saw puzzle pieces
have somehow snuck into the picture.
I'm starting to panic. I can feel a smile coming on
and I don't think I can keep my mouth shut much longer.

Everything old is new again and everything new is old
EVERYthing's hazy and fade, fading away,
and now EVERYthing's ... NOthing
and NOthing's ... fading ... fading out.

I know the whole thing is broken and that's fine.
I know I'm broken, and that's fine too.
My brain has been so very surreal and abstracted lately.
And the missing piece, even if I were able to find it,
wouldn't complete my jigsaw conundrum, and that's okay too.
You know I've always been that way ... puzzling.

A Conversation with Steven

Listen Steven.
You'll know it when you see it,
even if you can't explain it.

It could be:
Cleanly shaven.
Poorly shaven.
Evenly shaven.
Or unshaven ... even

It could be:
Night in the village.
Noon on the seashore.
Or dawn breaking, unevenly,
high atop the Himalayas ... even.

It could be:
Me running scared.
Scared running.
Unevenly running in circles.
Or stumbling down ... even.

It could be:
A twitching eye.
A glass nerve jumping.
A rubber heart thumping.
Or an elastic taut laxation ... even.

What it couldn't be is:
This poem being unread.
These breathing words being left for dead.
Me changing my name to Fred.
The world hanging by a thread ... even.

I can't explain it
but you'll know it when you see it.
In the dark ... even.

In the breathless eyes of death.
In the shivered skin crawl of a centurion ... even.

Even if I could, I wouldn't explain it.
But I would offer to buy you a drink.
And we could drink to the unspoken.
And I would offer you the contents of my wallet,
but not the rest of me.
because I'd rather lose money than mind.

Then we could discuss some far out concept
after thinking of the odd one ... even.

If, after doing all this,
you still don't catch a glimpse of it,
don't beat yourself up.
After all, they say many are called,
but the chosen are few.
And I'm still not sure what it is ... even.

If it's a blessing, a curse or worse ... even.
All I know is ... it's odd Steven.

Blue Herring

It's not to be taken too seriously.
It's not like that.
Is there an urgency to the thing?
Yes, of course.

But that's not the same as the red herring of too serious.
Not at all.

But it is as serious as the ever elusive blue herring.
I caught one once, but it slipped the hook
and slipped the frypan.
There was a poem there somewhere,
but it slipped my mind at the time
and now I can't get it back
except in bits of scales and skin.

Now... on to more serious things!
Do I want to publish 100 books
before the lights turn out?
Yes.
Do I want to believe the words
have enough pressure force to bust pipes?
Yes I do. 'Deed I do!
Do I want my contributions to be seen
as honest expressions coming from an original mind?
Sure, why not.

It's not to be taken too figuratively.
It's not like that.

Do the hills and valleys truly thwart the possibility
of a sustained pretense? They ought to.
Are the flames seen in the fire
the same thing as the stars seen in the sky?
In a Carl Jung kinda way ... for sure.

Is it best to maintain humor

regarding one's shortcomings?
Obviously.

Right now,
Carl is relaxing in his big, pie in the sky grey matter lab.

Me?
I'm still fishing for that blue herring I lost
and the poem I know is out there somewhere ...
Somewhere beyond the scales and the skin.

Evolver

Everything matters and nothing matters.
The Buddha view knows both to be accurate.
You will know both to be accurate as well
once you awaken and "come to" on this fortunate journey.

All movement is mutual and exacting
while maintaining its devout independence.
The quantum physicist knows both to be accurate.
You will know both to be accurate as well
once you hoist the white flag
and accept it's all just a game.

Tommy Edwards knew this way back in the 60s.
A crazy cool singa-man who romanced the mic,
crooning out "It's All in the Game"
He knew it. Back then he musta bin a closet Buddha
and Whudda thought it ... as thoughts go and come.
And my thought is ... when will my heart fly away?

Einstein, Bohm, Bohr tangled with spooky energy
Talbot scratched the edges of a holographic universe.
Greene danced to the harmonics of string theory.
Here but not here. Proof but not proof.

We are all just a tango of quantum entanglement
and spooky energy at a distance personified.
These things spook the hell out of me until they don't.
Buddha wound get it ... maybe you get it too.

Ok so check this out.
This one dude this one time told me that it's best
to take life one day at a time.
And that was good enough for me.
Until this other time, this other dude came to me
and said it's best to take life one step at a time.
And that's been good enough for me ever since.
I always take the sublime to the ridiculous

so I went out and bought some step ladders
and then I bought a stair stepper machine
but that still wasn't good enough.
I was afraid I might somehow be out of step
and worse yet possibly missing some steps ...
Steps I should have taken to ensure my pace
was in key and in touch with my grace.
I knew I had grace somewhere in me
and I was taking every step I could to find it.

And then I looked at the fresh dew on a leaf
And I saw it. I saw Buddha reflecting in that leaf.
It was at that moment that I asked him
'Why am I here?" What am I supposed to do?"

He wiped the sun from his brow
and the moonlight shone in his eyes.
He said in eloquent, rhythmic speech:
You are here for everything and nothing.
You are here to see the accurate and the inaccurate
You need to learn to balance the unbalanced.
But most of all you are here to learn
the depth and breadth of your breath
and become one with the lungs of the universe.

I saw the all in the one and the one in the all.
I saw everything in nothing and nothing in everything.
I was free! Free to fly away.

I was so enlightened by this conversation
I went home and threw away all my ladders.

I realized you can only reach the Dharma
with an open and pure energy of mind
and an imagination that keeps evolving
to eventually become *The Evolver*.

The Poem Lives

The first step is writing "untitled"
at the top of the page.
Next step is two-fold;
ensure there is a glass next to you
and also ensure it's full.
Now get the tattered scroll of loose leaf paper.
Yeah, that stack.
And sort of try to straighten the pages out,
but don't worry about this step too much.

Now take two big pulls from the chalice
that should be situated just off to your right.
Sit back just a bit in the chair
and take two deep belly breaths.
Then it's time.

Time for all the mixed up words
to square dance through your head
in a boot-scootin' boogie kind of groove
then circle back to the Ponderosa.
You know, that place you hang your hat
and your brain and your heart and the bod.

Right! Now pick up the scalpel/pen
and let the heat from your hand mosey-on-down
to the lines corralled on the tattered page.
You can see they are stark-naked empty
and you hear them wailing for ink,
so you set your poetic hand to the ready
for the delicate surgery you're about to perform.

You enter the theatre of poesy in gloves, gown and mask.
The room hangs heavy with a life and death atmosphere.
The overhead lights flash on, fab-flourescent bright.

The muse wipes the sweat from your brow
and hands you the invisible tools:
Scalpel, spreader, sponges, props.

The procedure progresses sporadic and smooth.

Then suddenly...it's over!

The theatre lights slowly dim,
you remove the skin from your hands
and peel the flesh from your body.

The operation's a success.
The poem lives!

Authors Profile

Jose & James are a rough and tumble, sensitive collaborative team, living off-planet. They are seekers and gatherers of obscure thoughts and bizarre moments in the quantum boiling pot of timeless time. When they are not writing poetry, their hobby is chasing nuclear butterflies with their collapsible net of poetry as they time travel through their air stream of ink and words, polishing their poems to a super-fine gloss and shine.

If you watch closely you may be able to see them flashing in and out of time on retrograde Moon rotational nights.

Mebbee ... Mebbee not.